King Cophetua

KING COPHETUA

Julien Gracq

TRANSLATED BY
Ingeborg M. Kohn

TURTLE POINT PRESS
NEW YORK

*Il faut
cultiver
notre
jardin*

2003

Le Roi Cophetua
Copyright © Librairie José Corti, 1970

ISBN 1-885586-86-8
LCCN 2002115169

Turtle Point Press
Room 946
233 Broadway
New York, N.Y. 10279

*W*hen I think of the time that marks the end of my youth, nothing seems more oppressive, more troubling, than the memory of those months during which ripened, without anyone realizing what was happening, the decision that brought World War I to a head. Thoughts of a period which bring to mind that bucket-brigade of earth-encrusted, worn out soldiers on leave from the front, with their grotesque gas masks and blue greatcoats whose flaps were folded up and held in place by a triangle of buttons to keep them from wearing out at the knees, who were drinking to each other's health, right out of their blue canteens – the lowest, poorest of the men fighting in the trenches, saddled with their potato sacks, talking in that dialect particular to the seasonal Flemish farm workers who come down from the North every year for the sugar beet harvest – a time which, now that the modern-style has regained a sort of cachet, is languishing in one of those in-between fashion zones whose representative samples seem to be just shop-worn dummies forgotten inside their display windows, waiting to gain access to the museum of costumes. Up towards the Northeast, sugar beets in the fields of the silt-covered plateaus sank deeper into the earth rather than grow upwards, but France, in 1917, still deeply anchored in its peasant roots and accustomed to enforced labor, braved the winds and rains before sinking into the mire, keeping up a routine which had become just as petty, small-time, and backwards as its war operations. In 1917, like the recurring images of the sower's noble gesture and the vintner's grape-laden cart – bumper crop or meager harvest – the war continued, plowing the earth in great shovelfuls, without worrying about useless justifications: one might even wonder whether or not it had ever started. Seen in hindsight, through the well-oiled routines of the changing of the guard, the mayor's visits to bereaved families, the seasonal levies on small savings accounts by the government to finance the war, the meticulous press releases at fixed hours, week after week, about the reconquest of a stand of trees or the loss of a cabbage patch, the war might be lacking in perspectives, but provided the modicum of spiritual necessities people needed to live while waiting for it to end: an acceptable image of order and stability.

However, as the years went by, fatigue had set in, a heavy fatigue like the one weighing down the foot-soldier who falls asleep while marching, but keeps on walking ahead, as if in a dream. I had been injured in the winter of 1914, during the Battle of Flanders, and then discharged; back at my job as a parliamentary journalist, I knew more about those dreams than what one read in the newspapers, where censorship each month added more white spaces, like patches on an old hospital blanket. The summer mutinies had ended, but the abscess continued to fester: the uprisings could resume any week. Worn out, the French Ministry agonized; talk in the hallways of the House had already pronounced it dead. Far away, Kerensky's Russia swirled enigmatically in the muddy streets of Moscow and Petrograd, like leaves blown sky-high before a thunderstorm; looking at photographs of streets published by the newspapers that showed crowds blown up by volleys of gunfire into something that looked like the star-studded nucleus of a comet or a cloud of sawdust, one could only decipher the molecular tension of an unknown species, but there was no structure for further reading: it was like a silent image of an explosion so far away that its sound waves had not yet reached us. For the first time, one had a vague feeling that this enormous killing spree of local interest was something which would lead somewhere beyond the hoisting of the Tricolore atop the spire of Strasbourg's cathedral. Now that the respite caused by the first onslaught of mud had slowed down the activities on the front lines, one could have said that the soul, numbed by the prolonged shock of crude images and worn out by years of violent blows, was wide open to premonitions, like hope caught in a dead end, and tried to read between the clouds breaking up on the horizon. The final shock was imminent: it was expected to happen in the spring – but that last season of waiting coming down with the November rains was filled with a deep fatigue and prophetic, joyless dreams, which rose from the laboured earth without warming it, like a dawn over the trenches.

Leaving Paris by train from the Gare du Nord on that afternoon of All Saints Day, through sheets of rain chased by the wind over factories and worker's weekend garden plots, the eye was drawn only to the suburban cemeteries, where riots of enormous floral offerings blotted out,

soaked up the black rain here and there – cemeteries submerged in, bristling with, dotted and
criss-crossed by the Tricolore, filled with crowds
dressed in badly dyed mourning clothes that cir-
culated slowly between the greenery like a flood of
soot, flecked here and there by spots of blue sky or
the white veil of a nurse, intersected by narrow
pathways opened up by crowds retreating in order
to let pass the tricycles maneuvered by amputees.
Never had the hitherto worst neglected, or quickly
forgotten civilian deceased been more tenderly
tucked in, taken care of, or visited more often than
during the big Memorial Days in honor of the
Dead in those years; they regained their youth,
drowned by proxy underneath a dazzling tide
which a dike of fire prevented from attaining the
trenches. Further out in the suburbs, these fiery
bushes which seemed to burn on the water died
out; the Tricolore showed up less often, just a
washed-out reminder here and there on the sentry
boxes of railway guards seen patrolling along the

bridge railings, men lost in the rain who had turned up their coat collars for protection against the downpour, and then we were in the country – the dreary countryside of the North dotted by its twin-building train stations made of sandstone, whose platforms seem to be larger and emptier than elsewhere, when deserted by the crowds returning from the racetracks.

I was alone in my compartment – almost alone, or so it seemed, in that slow-moving, aimless regional train winding its way through the greater suburbs – and the prospect of spending a day in the country seemed less and less appealing. The light started to fade very early – a colorless break in the low ceiling was gliding across the Western horizon, mirrored, here and there, in the large puddles covering the plowed fields – on the roads, the wind was chasing swarms of falling leaves. I stopped looking at the countryside gliding by motionless before my eyes, a landscape the color of dark graphite and wet tree bark, and briefly leafed through the newspapers I bought at the train station. The French Air Force had bombed the Kaiserslautern barracks during the night. Reading between the lines of the delicately phrased press releases, I gathered that the situation in Russia was getting worse. Cold humidity filtered through the badly fitting window into my compartment: I slid back into my corner, curled up in my coat, and began to drowse. I imagined Petrograd, the frozen tide of its red flags suddenly blackened by the first snowfall, millions of heavy boot steps trampling round and round like those of barrack inmates gone mad, ruining the melted snow plastered with newsprint. A detour through the marshes of Yser reminded me of the black winter just now starting at the front lines: civilian life had reclaimed me, memories of gunfire had already receded into another world, but each time the autumn rains returned, I still *felt* the trenches in spite of myself, like someone afflicted with rheumatism in his inflamed joints. Once more, the wet cold gripped my wrists; the train, which carried no one to the front lines, stopped endlessly at every station. It was almost impossible to imagine a gloomier place, or a day more dreary than this one; it seemed as though the whole world was slowly turning moldy in this spongy wetness, and that I was sinking along with it into a nightmarish swamp, its color like those brackish waters in gravel pits where animals float belly-up. Nevertheless, from time to time a wave of curiosity welled up inside of me like a warm little flame, cutting through that deluge of dampness: I was thinking that soon I would see Jacques Nueil again.

I did not know him well. In the years preceding the war, I used to see him now and then in the press room of a daily newspaper where he briefly occupied the post of music critic, in concert halls, and at aviation meetings held on sun-scorched fields in the suburbs where he invited me to accompany him — wearing goggles, long gloves, swathed in a suit designed to protect its wearer from the dust – driving one of those superbly distinguished *coupés* which now grace automobile museums. He changed models every year. His silhouette came alive among my memories as did the bustle of the Paris street which had, almost every time, thrown him onto my path like a revolving door – together with the shimmering air over the roads to Deauville at summertime, where the first fast cars left trails of exhaust smoke between the apple trees. The war had not ended this budding friendship, casually begun and loosely kept up, which revived and reanimated itself almost spontaneously, set aflutter like a scarf in a breeze. From time to time, I would receive short, ironic, very affected letters from him, without a hint of frontline seriousness, where the tone remained strictly *Parisian*. The French Air Force had recruited its first fighter pilots among those *sportsmen* of 1910 – men with a touch of anglomania, a little snobbish, speaking among themselves a secret language, who had entered the machine age like one enters religion – blazing their trails through the French heartland like forerunners of an exotic fauna, setting themselves apart from the others by their roars, their odor. But until now Nueil had survived, transferred just in time, after a landing accident, into one of the VOISIN night bomber squadrons who once in a while dropped their bombs on train stations and factories of the Palatinate without doing any noticeable damages. Opening one of his letters was like a warm breeze gently blowing into my face. It brought back – quite clearly – memories of a pre-war period now lost, where summers were sunnier than ever, already abuzz with fragile insects made from wood and cloth, so strangely prophetic, but an era still young, joyous, windswept, adventurous, *detached* like no other, where the roads of France beckoned with a freshness never seen before, and which still comes alive for me, oddly enough, in Apollinaire's poems as well as in the waggish verses of Arsene Lupin, or images of Maurice Chevalier wearing the newly fashionable sailor hat, set jauntily over one eye.

There existed another Nueil whom I hardly knew; the composer who hid his music, but nevertheless was being talked about by people in circles far removed from that of *looping the loop* – the man who sequestered himself for long periods of time in his villa in the greater suburbs where I was now going for the first time. Granted a short leave, he had invited me by telegram to join him there, where he himself would arrive on this afternoon of All Saints' Day. I pulled the already crumpled blue rectangular paper from my pocket, and verified once more the date of our rendezvous: detecting in it a trace of that somber humor he was known to affect. For the first time, I wondered whether he lived alone in his secret villa. Glancing briefly through the window, I noticed a squall brewing above the darkened countryside. The train was now rolling between the trees, having entered the first of many woods which border the

Valois region, and, in spite of the rain, views of the ancient royal forest where train tracks slide along trenches of leaves made me breathe easier; having left the noise of Paris behind, we now traveled across these noble, pristine forests standing guard against the encroachment of city life like a curtain of initiatory silence, behind which the ear, listening half-heartedly, already expected to hear *another* noise. Once again, an awareness of the war swept over me from far away on the rainy horizon, and I raised my hand in a gesture of annoyance, trying to chase it away as one would a wasp.

When I stepped off the train on the deserted platform at Braye-La-Forêt, suitcase in hand, a strong wind assailed me from all sides. The squall had dissipated, and I realized that it was still early afternoon; suddenly, the air was a lot clearer. Instead of the stormy gusts of wind, a powerful, steady breeze was blowing in from the sea, chasing armfuls of fallen leaves, still green, across the platform: behind the little buildings of the railroad station, over which towered trees of great height, an enormously loud, grating noise swept in wave after wave so that the platform, as soon as a stand of trees had swallowed the departing train at the next bend, looked suddenly emptier than a lonely seashore. No one was waiting for me. After passing through the side gate I put my suitcase down for a few moments and listened, almost intimidated, to the roar of the sea churning masses of green foam, then tried to orient myself. There was not a soul in sight. In front of me, a wall of porous stone topped by bricks ran along a narrow road that looked like a bridle path, full of weeds and yellow mud, dotted by wind-stirred puddles. Everywhere, swarms of leaves blown by the wind filled the air; the odor of the soaked, acrid, but still green November paths permeated the length and width of the road. I felt strangely alone between those forbidding walls above which the upper branches of hedges and arbours, furiously battered by the wind like a row of bushes along a dike, welled and lashed out against each other with the violence of a heavy swell.

Braye-la-Forêt was evidently one of those villages built up close against the ancient royal forests where Parisians eager to breathe fresh air had begun to settle and colonize: an ancient hamlet reminiscent of grand culture caught in the circle of a fretful solitude common to enclaves of weekend residents. After winding its way briefly between the walls of parks left to grow wild, where rusty iron gates, flowerbeds choked by weeds, and mounds of leaves undisturbed by rakes pointed to the long, dead season of war, the alley unexpectedly turned into a narrow village street where footsteps resounded briefly on a paved sidewalk; I was now walking between two rows of small houses built side by side, asleep behind their green shutters underneath the short, reddish roof tiles common to the Valois region. After having walked past the school, past the church less tall than the trees around it, the tobacco shop and the café, the wall running all around the parks again joined that of a barn, an outpost whose tall gates, tightly shut, brought to a close this side of the village. Gusty winds had taken possession of the road just as easily as a mountain stream its bed of stones; in order to get directions, I had to ring for a long time at the door of one of the little houses. Then, once again, only sudden gusts of wind kept me company in the maze of trees inside the private parks. The branches joining each other above my head dripped monotonously; marching along, I started to shake the ice-cold drops off my neck with mechanical shrugs, like a chicken. But little by little my bad mood caused by this rain-soaked excursion started to fade. The solitude of the villas buried under branches was so imposing that my stride became both lighter and longer in spite of myself; it seemed as if I were coming to the end of that sleepy hollow lost underneath drifts of leaves to wake up something buried deep inside.

The villa La Fougeraie, with its densely

wooded park extending far behind it, was the last of the dwellings built against the forest; beyond its iron gates, the alley became a muddy path with deep ruts dug by foresters' vehicles, which plunged headlong into a dense beech grove covering the ravine; the same low wall built of silex and sandstone, which everywhere here shielded all the properties ensconced within so defiantly from prying eyes, isolated it from the path. Before ringing the doorbell, I passed in front of the gate and took a few steps up to the corner of the park, where the trodden path plunged head-on into the gully. On this side, the wall enclosing the property met, at a right angle, a retaining wall that ran along the beginning of the gully; an arbour bordered the terrace built up against it. The clipped hedges, the trimmed linden trees contrasted markedly with the neglected parks all around Braye, but this sealed-off terrace without any view, set squarely against the trees of the ravine evoked more vividly than any other the idea of a dead end, an outpost stuck like a foreign object inside the thick forest. It was clear to see that right here the war had put a stop to the construction of vacation homes encroaching on the woods. Little by little, the forest was now reclaiming its terrain; swirls of blowing leaves patrolling unchecked through the alleys, trees growing wild over walls and fences made one think of those domestic animals who start to bristle, fur standing on end, when they hear the calls of their savage brothers approaching. Standing on this clearing about to be swallowed by the wilderness, I suddenly felt utterly alone. I even began to doubt that anyone was expecting me here. Reaching for the doorbell, hesitating to announce myself, I listened once more, intimidated, to a strong gust of wind that bent low the trees bordering the alley. The ringing of the bell from the depths of that drenched woodland seemed strangely out of season.

The movement of the silhouette in front of me – one of her feet barely touching the ground –

was quite lively and yet seemed to be suspended in mid-air, as if surprised by someone unexpectedly taking a snapshot of her: seeing that I hesitated, a sudden awareness, rather than a smile, lit up her eyes for an instant, as if touched lightly by a delicate sensor.

– Yes, Mr. Nueil is expecting you this afternoon. But he has not arrived yet.

The attentiveness in her almond-shaped eyes disappeared, she apparently did not want to say more. Only the noise of our footsteps, side by side, resounded on the wet gravel. But, once inside its walls, I hardly paid attention to the soaked garden where the noise of the storm seemed much quieter; walking along, I was strangely aware of that lively step next to mine.

Leaving behind the curtain of trees that rose above the garden wall, we crossed a formal English garden where the gravel, in spite of the downpour, still showed the marks of a rake. At the other end of that wide-open space stood the villa, visible from the gate, though already half-hidden by the foliage of trees that towered over it, trees belonging to a park which lay immediately behind it. The building stretched out in all its length underneath the trees. Half of the facade was of a rather light and airy construction; it consisted of a single-story structure that featured a series of large bay windows overlooking the garden – an architectural element still rare at that time – which evoked an almost aggressive modernity, contrasted by the site's seclusion; it seemed as though those oversized bay windows, some of them without curtains, called for a setting and a light which the mournful twilight of the park refused to provide. Rather than suggesting a permanently inhabited residence, the eye was reminded of those secluded lodges or discreetly luxurious vacation homes not so easily accessible, wide open to the summer air and shaded by trees, built for a special clientele who belongs to the horse racing set or fashionable golf clubs, but which at the onslaught of winter – looking rusty, washed out, faded – suddenly resemble a luxury liner run aground beneath the branches of a cove far out on the seashore.

The room where I was taken must have been a combination salon, smoking parlor, and music room, or rather a study, because it was obvious that Nueil used to write his compositions here. A grand piano and an upright occupied the entire left side of the room; the music cabinets separating them contained bound partitions and reams of lined composing paper. But this most intimate corner of the room lacked that feeling of lively disorder associated with daily work. While I tilted the carefully classified partitions with my fingertips in order to read the titles, or ran my fingers over the piano top devoid of the slightest speck of dust, the image which crystallized in my mind became cold, even glacial: it was the image of one of those residences converted into museums where, in the corner of a room the visitor is passing through, a drawn chain and posted sign isolate the table, the chair, the inkwell, the sharpened quills consecrated long ago by an illustrious hand, a scene where disorder, dutifully dusted, is no longer animated by life, but frozen in time by rigor mortis. This side of the room, lit only by a great wooden fire, was already half plunged into darkness. To the East, the spacious bay windows, separated by a French door, looked out over the lawn in the direction of the arbour that I had seen from the path. On this side, the eye was drawn towards the treetops before coming to rest on the slope that overlooked the gully; on the left side, one could imagine the leafy borders of the little park. It seemed as if the forest was closing in from all sides on the raked, sand-strewn clearing: the sounds of the sea swept over it like waves on an autumn seashore. From time to time, an isolated gust of wind slammed a mass of leaves against the trembling windowpanes; in spite of the fire, an atmosphere of isolation and wet cold permeated the room;

darkness had already started to engulf the space below the ceiling which reflected the flames dancing in the fireplace, but there was still enough daylight coming through the bay windows to cast a feeble shine on the parquet floor gleaming between the carpets, the copper lamp bases, the varnished piano top. The vast, empty room was getting ready for the night, and I hardly felt at ease. It was difficult to believe that someone, at this hour, could *come home* here.

While looking out the window to see the daylight fade over the soggy park, I listened closely from time to time. Not a single noise coming from inside the house was heard in this room, although it seemed so receptive to sounds; it was as though I had been left all alone in the house. Tired from pacing to and fro, I sat down in an armchair in the corner next to the fireplace, and, while halfheartedly stirring the logs, I reopened, for lack of something else to do, the morning paper still in its envelope on top of the music cabinet. Once again, rather absentmindedly, I read the press release, when – like the insistent ringing of a telephone in a distant room suddenly forces someone half asleep to wake up and take notice – the name Kaiserslautern made a noticeable dent in my consciousness. I held the paper closer to the firelight and smoothed the pages with a nervous hand. The habitual announcement that all deployed airplanes had come back was missing. I quickly unfolded the paper bought at the train station; the short, reassuring sentence was also missing, a small annoyance like a misplaced key. This was not a printer's mistake.

I tried to control my nervousness. But with the onset of night, the silence of the room sinking into darkness became oppressive; I needed air. I opened the French doors and walked the short distance to the arbour on the wet gravel crunching beneath my feet. Outside, there was still a faint glimmer of daylight; below the canopy of clouds on the Western horizon a bright shaft of light had opened up between the trees and the arbour. The wind was now colder – every so often, strong gusts shook the branches and swept over the forest, like a mocking gesture falsely announcing a return of good weather – but it was one of those sudden quiet spells which made me stop momentarily in my tracks and listen attentively. There was no doubt about it; this rumbling that accompanied quiet nights like an accomplice, a sound heard all the way from Flanders which the distance evened out like the summits of a faraway mountain range, I knew it well.

It was not all that unexpected. Softened, already flattened out by the distance, it was not even particularly sinister. After many months during which its absence must have sharpened my ear a little, it was simply here again; the schoolboys of Braye-la-Forêt, returning home after school late in the afternoon, knew at which turn of the road they would hear it again. Head a little dizzy, legs heavy, I stopped dead in my tracks, and listened to it. Coming very clearly from the North, carried by a sharp, dry wind that swept the avenues in advance of its chariot's rumblings. With night falling, the earth was prepared for the onslaught of its sounds, ready to be jolted. I went back into the salon in a changed mood. The noise followed me inside through the open French doors, among the mirrors and varnished furniture, as familiarly as a dog accustomed to scamper in on muddy paws, ears flopping, wagging his tail. I switched on the light, lit a cigarette and then, irritated, turned my back to the already dark bay windows while taking a rather desultory inventory of the library shelves' contents. A more brutal blast of wind bent the trees of the park very low to the sound of branches cracking, and breaking; all the lights went out. Surprised by the sudden darkness, I slid back into the armchair, gripping its side supports, and waited for a moment without budging. The rumbling of the gunfire now filled the pitch-black room with an intimate presence: strong enough at times to elicit faint tinkling sounds from the Venetian glass figurines set close to each other on the mantelpiece. I found it odd to be left so utterly alone in that house lost in its dreams, but remained seated, motionless, for a long time. Ever since childhood I have always loved the way a house all closed and shuttered is settling into dusk – just as I am attracted to the troubling sensations felt at low tide, when a strange feeling of momentary release animates the empty rooms just before the lamps are lit. I listened to the delicate chiming of the glass on the mantelpiece, and to the steady ticking of the clock which, little by little, the onset of darkness had rescued from being drowned out by daytime noises. Reflected in the mirror over the mantelpiece facing me, I could see the gradual fading of a last patch of daylight the color of silvering. The oppressive daytime hours were coming to an end, but what followed was not exactly nighttime: rather, it seemed to be – steady and calm like a small candle flickering in the midst of rooms sound asleep – much more like a vigil.

There is nothing more alive, nothing more suddenly and reassuringly maternal during a dark night in the country when the electricity has been cut, than that heartwarming first flicker of candlelight whose reflection lights up and flows along the wall, just as if the home's heartbeat had been restored. Overcome by a feeling of well-being, I watched for a moment that light come alive at the far end of the hallway, then jumped up and walked towards the door. It would have been embarrassing if someone had found me reclining in the darkness.

It took a few seconds before I recognized the woman who had led me into this room, and then the same wave of attention, alertness, and surprise swept over me, even more acute this time. At first I saw only the silhouette of her bare arm partially covered by the end of a shawl – carrying, as I noticed once she had stepped over the threshold, a two-armed candelabra in a gesture both gracious and intangibly theatrical. Behind the small flecks of trembling lights only her eyes and lips shone brightly – the heavy cascade of black hair was lost in the enlarged shadow thrown on the wall. The gesture of the arm remained suspended in the air, with just a hint of dreamy complacency, a second longer than needed to find the table – not unlike someone trying to illuminate the face of a sleeping patient, or a night patrol verifying the presence of a prisoner.

– I am late, she said finally – please excuse me. The tone of voice was that of a dutiful chambermaid, which clashed with the strange gesture of the raised arm carrying a candelabra. – This happens quite often now. It is because of the branches that need cutting.

– Lieutenant Nueil has not arrived yet?

She did not answer, but only shook her head and shoulders in a movement that again seemed surprising: this time, her gesture suggested a certain panic. More veiled refusal than response, it blocked me momentarily out of her field of vision.

– I don't think I misread his telegram. He invited me to come this afternoon.

There was a brief moment of silence.

– Yes, she said without looking at me, in a toneless voice. – He must have been delayed.

The silhouette melted into the dark hallway; once again, I found myself alone. The atmosphere of the mournful room, its windows now opaque, had become more oppressive. Only the reflection of a shiny lacquered panel of furniture pierced the room's shadows for an instant or two, stirring, or so it seemed, the thick gray tufts of the deep pile wool carpet – from time to time, a more luminous ray projected a shard of light into the tall, frameless mirror at the far end of the room. I reached up to a bookshelf to take down a novel which had just been published; brand-new, with its pages still uncut, it resembled this lifeless room frozen in time, but I could not concentrate my attention on what I was reading. I picked up the newspaper that had fallen on the carpet and started to leaf through it once more, as if I had somehow skipped a news item of importance to me. The light of the candle glided over the paper without illuminating it, like a feeble fluttering of wings. Again, the newspaper slid to the floor, and I settled back into an armchair. My mind a blank, I observed the tip of the flame stretching its smoky tendrils into the darkness. The rumbling continued to roll in through the half-open French doors leading into the park – while I, at some distance from the hallway, ears strained to the utmost, was trying to catch noises emanating from the inner regions of the house. Where had this woman disappeared? I was not really wondering who she was, or what she was doing here. To be left alone, abandoned in such a manner, was no longer a surprise. At times, I even stopped wondering about Nueil. I was thinking of that mass of black hair, those thick tresses so very much alive in that gloomy house.

When the delicate chime of a clock on the mantelpiece struck seven from deep within the obscurity, I stood up, taking hold of the candelabra whose small yellow flames flickered very low; at the other end of the room, the mirror and the shiny surface of the grand piano caught the light's reflection and started to come alive. The thin metallic strokes had awakened me from my daydreams; even before having reached a decision about what to do next, I found myself walking down the hall. The house was as dark as a mineshaft. I advanced without making a sound, my steps muffled by the plush wall-to-wall carpeting; once or twice, intimidated by the silence, I struck the handle of the candelabra, noisily and deliberately, against a piece of furniture. I passed in front of a flight of stairs which disappeared above me into a cavern of shadows; curious, I went up a few steps and swept the candlelight above me for an instant; once again, the reflection was caught by a mirror which came to life up ahead on the landing, casting a feeble light on some copper railings; just like in the salon, everything here seemed to be varnished, cold, deserted; a late-night stroll through a big department store would not have brought to light anything more lifeless and more anonymous. Rather undecided, I continued along the hallway which turned at a right angle towards a side wing. It seemed as if behind me, in the wake of the trail of light gliding along the walls, an icy frost was again settling in the house. I began to wonder whether I had been left all alone, when I noticed on my right the rectangle of an open door.

At first glance, after holding the candelabra across the threshold into the room, I thought nobody was there. The room, its floor tiled in black and white, looked empty; only the corner of a table, which might have been that of a pantry, protruded out of the darkness. Then, once the light of the candles illuminated the room, I was able to make out the contours of a shelf facing me from which came the tick-tock of an alarm clock, a sewing basket on a wicker stand, and, at the other end of the table, seated, motionless, the woman who had led me inside this house.

Her face was turned towards me and her forearms raised into mid-air as if surprised by the sudden burst of light, but this interrupted gesture did not blot out the image perceived a second or so beforehand when, elbows resting on the table, her face had been buried in the palms of her hands. The expression in her somber, burning eyes, unmercifully exposed by the light, was so clearly an expression of being utterly *lost* that I put the candelabra on the table with a gesture of respectful discretion: her face was again hidden in darkness, but she immediately began to speak, as if spurred by a defense mechanism, like a woman surprised while getting dressed who instinctively raises her arms to cover her breasts.

– Dinner will be ready right away. I did not have enough candles. I am sorry that you had to wait.

– Dinner is out of the question. Lieutenant Neuil is not coming, and to wait much longer would be an indiscretion. Something must have prevented him.

– No! The voice was low, almost a whisper – the intimate light of the candles lowering the tone of voice instinctively; I was startled by its musical and sensual qualities, and by the beseeching accent underneath: suddenly, for the first time, I had the acute feeling that we were alone with each other in this dark house: – There are no more trains at this hour at the Braye train station, she added hurriedly, with her voice lowered, which emphasized the pitiful falsehood of her statement.

– What should I do?

– Don't you want to wait? once again, there was that beseeching tone in her voice, so difficult to resist.

– All right. . . . I replied after a short hesitation: making up my mind seemed easy. – Dinner it shall be. . . . Don't you want to keep the light? I continued, somewhat embarrassed; I felt sorry for her, and intimidated. It is so dark in the house.

– Yes . . . the simplest monosyllables took on a weighty, almost carnal significance in that mouth; neither acceptance nor refusal, but rather, or so it seemed, every time it was both exorcism and avowal: the *no* like a surge of an intimate panic; the *yes* like a confident, warm reaffirmation. She stood up and reached for a simple candle holder on the shelf; I tilted my candelabra and lit her candle with mine; on the wall a warmer light spread out in a wave, and we smiled for an instant, eyes fixed on each other, faces turned towards the light, as if clinking glasses before taking a drink.

– I will call you in an instant, she said in that same low and monotonous tone of voice . . . – There is no reason to worry.

Once again I found myself in that somber salon. The sound of gunfire seemed to shatter the side of the room lying in total darkness. It was as if the house was split in two, like those villas built on the edge of a wilderness facing the seashore. Behind the tidal storm which battered the walls and shook the windows, I could still feel distinctly that unexpected, cloistered softness of the house's inner regions on the other side of the hallway, a silent night closing in around itself, an ancient night that seemed to pour forth from wardrobes along with their age-old perfumes. Who was that woman? In the limited register available to us where we tend to classify women we have met, her behaviour did not strike a chord. The impersonal deference of her utterances, the way she showed up only when her services were needed, made me think of a simple chambermaid, but not that manner in which, so directly, so unconventionally, and almost indiscreetly, she suddenly seemed to exist only for you. A distant relative in charge of the household would have spoken more freely, mentioned Nueil by his given name. The conventional idea of the *servant-mistress* floated up in my imagination, made me momentarily purse my lips ironically. While my mind vacillated without conviction from one possibility to another, there was one image to which I was magnetically drawn, an image that made me forget instantly any need to *situate* her: that face hidden by her hands, in a corner of the dark room.

At times, the rumble of the gunfire battered the windows with the heaviest of blows. Night did not abolish the distance, it only rendered it abstract and almost immaterial; as though there was nothing left between me and that relentless pounding on the door. The feeling of isolation, which had taken hold of me as soon as I set foot on the platform at the train station, became a bizarre daydream. Paris suddenly seemed very far away, cut off by those drenched forests, by that black, raging storm: I had a strange feeling that I was standing on an ill-defined border. Abandoned in *a no man's land* – one of those zones in the process of being evacuated, from which the authorities are already moving out, but where the enemy has not yet penetrated. I thought with uneasiness of those villas around me, closed and shuttered tightly now for years inside their overgrown parks, surrounded by puddles, scraped by tree branches – listening from within silence as deep as a black pond to the deceitful alerts sounded by their trembling windowpanes. At certain moments, when a shift of the wind pushed the sound of gunfire aside like a curtain, I listened to the storm raging in the trees, which had resumed after the lull, picking up strength for the bad night still ahead. *La mala noche*. . . . These words came to mind, opening up a stream of thoughts. In the trembling twilight of the candles, images slipped in and out without resistance; suddenly, the memory of an etching by Goya blotted out all others. Against a dark background of black graphite, two women emerge from the stormy night: one black form, the other white. What is happening on that lonely moor, in the middle of that moonless night: Sabbath – kidnapping – infanticide? All the forbidden, disputed elements of this nocturnal meeting seem to have taken cover underneath the heavy, billowing skirts of the child ravisher's black silhouette, and in her shadowed face with its Mongolian, impassible traits and slanted, heavy-lidded eyes. But the light of the limestone which sharply outlines the white silhouette against the night, and the furious wind blowing a light-colored petticoat high up on her hips, revealing perfect legs, wind that whips her veil like a flag and outlines the draped contours of a shoulder and a charming head, are entirely the forces of desire. The veiled face, turned towards the night, is looking at something which cannot be seen; the posture does not suggest fear, fascination, or stupor. One is confronted by the savage anonymity of desire; but that denuded and flagellated silhouette, which nevertheless maintains triumphantly some kind of elegance *lost*, and that brutal wind which slaps the veil over her eyes and mouth and bares the thighs, hints at a worse kind of temptation.

No one came. Once again, I rose from the armchair and strained my ears; no noise emanated from within the house, all I could hear was the occasional clinking, clear thud of a fallen roof tile, and the sound of the wind ransacking the deserted courtyard. I took a few steps out of the room into the dark garden. The rain had stopped, but the wind immediately assailed me from all sides – the fallen leaves flew about by handfuls in the thick darkness. Out in the open air, the deep rumbling coming from the North stabilized into a strange monotony: trying to listen to it across the shifting storm – now settled on the horizon – the ear, though straining to the utmost, was unable to perceive any change of frequency or volume, like eyes staring at a blank wall. The idea that Nueil could still arrive suddenly seemed absurd. It was now impossible to believe that anything alive could come forth from that cataract of noise, that horizon about to disintegrate. A squall of rain burst behind me in the garden, above the invisible arbour. While I hurriedly walked back to the stairs in front of the entry, I suddenly realized that something was already leading me back to a familiar track; my eyes started to follow the sway of a dancing light that projected itself from inside the rear part of the house against the wall of the courtyard.

When I think back to that rained-out, gloomy All Saints Day, nothing seems more essential to me than trying to recapture its exact lighting; I always felt that nothing could have happened as it did without that fragile, threatened intimacy, that atmosphere of a peaceful revelation so dreamlike and yet so ominous, made possible by the trembling candlelight. There were moments when powerful gusts of wind forced the hinges of the doors with such violence that the small flames flickered very low, sending a wave of shadows bouncing on the flatness of the walls. But the night was not altogether menacing. The flames blown low flickered without dying, like those tall tufts of grass whose roots resist the current of a babbling brook: a small source of light, alive and unfailing, a warm and protected cocoon around which night was opening. The eye of the storm was in this Japanese-like room with its glass partitions – so vulnerable – where the flickering light created a play of light and shadows, a theater of the unreal. When, from a balcony at nighttime, the eye strays across the street into a lighted room where the curtains have not been drawn, one sees silhouettes which seem to float as if on waters, barely stirring, moving around just as incomprehensibly as chess pieces in the aquarium of that unknown interior. An invisible door swallows them one by one until the last silhouette is rambling around all alone, from which the eye can no longer detach itself; it seems to have fallen prey suddenly to some measured and calm delirium;

the heart starts to beat faster while the eye fixes the sometimes abrupt, sometimes peaceful gestures of this human *ludion*, who goes about his affairs inside those glassed-in fluids as if spurred on by a hand touching the partition from time to time. It seemed as though I myself was in one of these destabilizing optical boxes, both inside and outside at the same time. I waited. I stopped reading. The flame of a candle has the same effect on a vacant stare as an Arabic chant has on our ears; it bewitches us with its extended high notes which dissolve into sudden gurgling, flute-like tones, before resuming its unifying, monotonous melody, steadfast enough to lean upon. For a moment the image of Braye-la-Forêt floated back into my mind, with its wet, slightly meandering main street, its rounded cobblestones dating back to a France still ruled by kings; I vividly recalled how impressed I had been by the ancient forest, its trees three times as tall as the low houses lined up in a double row, trees whose branches thrashed blindly into each other above the red-tiled roofs. It was like a village at the mercy of the sea, with its frothing forest ready to surge across the dike at any moment in a sort of revenge of the elements. And yet I knew that in the heart of the isolated village, hidden deep within that stormy afternoon, there was some kind of tranquil, protected haven. I looked at the reflection of the moving light which was again gliding along the wall in the hallway, coming from somewhere deep inside the house.

The room where the table had been set for me was smaller than the music room, but on its floor, as apparently elsewhere in the house, there was the same plush carpeting, which silenced every footstep. The tablecloth covered only the center of a long table, its surface as shiny as the mirror-gloss polish on the pianos in the salon. Between the two windows overlooking the park, above a sideboard where the candlelight coaxed the reflections of silverware from a frozen sleep, hung a long, low, slightly tilted mirror framed only by a simple black baguette, but so bright and so perfectly transparent to the very edges that the simplicity of the frame appeared to be, upon close inspection, only a discretion imposed around a precious matter; the small objects in the room reflected themselves in it with the haunting precision found in those somber interiors depicted by Dutch intimist painters. With the exception of a Chinese rug where dark blue designs were woven into a pattern resembling a coffered ceiling, the room was startlingly bare even for the taste of the times, a stark and impersonal bareness vaguely reminiscent of luxurious staterooms on an ocean liner, or of a suite in a grand hotel.

I dined in deep silence. As soon as I was alone, all I could hear was the faint tinkling of the trembling figurines on the tray set on the sideboard. From time to time, a creaking sound made by some of the furniture gave the impression that it was awakening from a museum's sleep, as if the house had been closed down for three years. I was not hungry. I still felt that constriction in my throat, which had gripped me as soon as I entered the house. But my uneasiness was fading, my premonitions no longer worried me as much. I could not stop looking in the tall mirror facing me – I was anticipating the moment when, behind me, the rectangle of the door would again frame the woman entering the room.

She was indeed a servant: there was no longer any doubt, because she had tied an apron around her waist and pinned a white cap on her hair. And yet, the mind took notice of that appearance but grudgingly; those touches abruptly added to her dress stood out, they were so severe, almost insolent in their humiliating correction that I wondered whether they were part of the service, or rather a sort of ceremony emphasized at will; she seemed to be making an appearance now, at her hour, as a servant, to ease back into some kind of intimidating freedom of movements, like a ruler casting off his disguise. The light of the candelabra which she had put on the table in front of me accentuated in a bizarre fashion the ritual character of these white ornaments in which she seemed to have dressed up, rather than put on customarily. Whenever she stood in front of the sideboard, bent slightly forward, her back turned for a moment, her long legs, pearl-white underneath black silk stockings, further emphasized the haughty character of the silhouette. A red arrow rising from the Achilles tendon drew attention to the stockings' area of reinforcement around the heel.

She entered without making a sound, the noise of her footsteps absorbed by the carpeting that covered the hallway, and I kept watching the mirror to catch the intense, cautiously watchful look in her almond-shaped eyes – further elongated by the eyeliner towards the temples – a look that crossed mine for an instant in the mirror. She served me, eyes lowered, with a neutral and grave precision, neither hastily nor slowly. She did not speak. Something in her attitude dissuaded me from addressing myself to her during those moments. It was as if she alone had been delegated to serve me – silently, hierarchical, headdress in place – one from a group of women who, according to feminine rituals depicted in miniature paintings of the Middle Ages, are shown waiting beyond the drawbridge to help the Knight-errant remove his armor, bathe him, serve him food. And yet, the feeling of her presence, when she entered the room for a moment and went about her business, could not for an instant be ignored: silent orders made her gestures flow, endowed her body with a troubling nearness. Whenever she approached to serve me, even at a distance from the faint yet vital warmth of her bare arm, I instantly felt a burning sensation on the back of my hand.

As soon as she had disappeared for a moment, I again succumbed to the monotonous, boring noise; I looked at the dimly lit tips of tree branches brushing against the windowpanes. The bareness of the room was broken only by a single painting of rather small dimensions, which took up the center of the wall to my left. The light of the candles did not illuminate it well; at first glance one could see only a somber rectangle. I took advantage of a moment when the servant had left the room to get up and hold the candelabra close to the wall. I did not want to be surprised; I was already afraid to interrupt the somber charm of this silent dinner.

The colors of the painting were dark, and the cover of yellowed, cracked varnish which must have been applied in successive layers had evened out and drowned the atelier browns, giving it a faded, melted aspect that aged it, although it was evident that the very conventional execution — which would not have been out of place in a salon during the times of Grévy or Carnot — was hardly ancient. I had to hold the candelabra very close to the painting to make out its subject. From the darkness covering the right corner, at the bottom of the painting, little by little there detached itself a figure wearing a purple coat, its face tanned by the sun, the forehead adorned with a coarse crown, down on bended knee with his head lowered in the posture of one of the Three Kings. In front of him, to the left, there stood – very erect, but head lowered – a young girl, almost a child, with bare arms, bare feet, hair falling over her shoulders. Head bent down low, face lost in the shadows, the iconical verticality of the silhouette bore a vague resemblance to some Virgin of the Visitation, but she was dressed only in some torn, dusty, white rags, which nevertheless brought to mind vividly, though it seemed ridiculous, the idea of a wedding dress. I could hardly imagine what might have frozen these two silhouettes into a state of such unbearable, silent paralysis. A tension difficult to identify animated the inexplicable scene: shame and burning confusion, panic; tension which seemed to rely on the deep twilight of the painting for some kind of protection – an avowal beyond words – an ignoble yet happy surrender – a bewildered acceptation of the inconceivable. I remained for a moment in front of the painting, my mind racing, conscious of the fact that it would be difficult to figure this one out. The face of the Moorish king made me think of Othello, but nothing in Desdemona's history evoked the malaise of this sordid annunciation. No. Not Othello. And yet, it was Shakespeare after all ... *King Cophetua!* King Cophetua in love with a beggar woman ...

When King Cophetua loved the beggar maid.

She came back sooner than anticipated; her silhouette was already framed by the doorway when I hastily sat down again at the table, causing the candles to flicker and their shadows to lurch on the wall. For a split second, she seemed to freeze on the threshold, steps suspended in mid-air, before starting to glide again on the carpet with that silent movement so particular to her. When she entered, she filled the room like a wave – carried, swept along by the wind – light yet substantial, eyes heavy and downcast. She had seen me, and for a split second was taken aback, aware of my action, but showing neither confusion nor embarrassment. Ever since she opened the garden gate for me, there had never been a gesture that did not seem to say: – This is how things are.

After finishing dinner, my uneasiness grew. It was becoming impossible to keep on waiting for news in that house which was sinking silently into night, oblivious to everything. I went back to the music salon, and picked up the telephone: the dial tone vibrated for a long time in my ear, an empty noise just as insignificant as the endless, frozen sound of an electric bell heard trembling during winter's early dawn at train stations in remote rural areas. The connection was apparently cut: in spite of the late hour, I decided to go to the post office and try to find out if a call had come for La Fougeraie; besides, the cold air might do me good. The rain had ceased, the storm was abating: from time to time, when the wind suddenly stopped blowing, one could hear the splatter of heavy rain-drops shaken off by trees towering over the walls. A misty drizzle filled the somber roads. Water gurgled everywhere around the stones in the road which covered a thick layer of fallen leaves – above me, visible through an opening in the ceiling of branches, patches of murky, flabby clouds glided underneath the ink-blotter sky which had cleared up a little, clouds so low they seemed to weigh down the line of tree tops. From time to time, I stopped and stood still for a few seconds, taking deep breaths of air filled with the odor of raw earth that rose in the night, listening to the far-away thunder, a sound very much like a heavy wave pounding against the shore, almost natural, almost peaceful. I felt strangely lost, adrift, sud-denly very far away from any kind of mooring.

The post office was located just a few steps away from the main street, on one of those short side streets bordered briefly by the walls of parks and by a rudimentary sidewalk made of trampled earth, but which almost immediately become paths leading into the forest. A small building of yellow sandstone with all its shutters closed, it sat among the trees like a forester's cabin: rain puddles soaked up the yellow mud of the sidewalk which came to an end ten meters further on. The place seemed so remote that, not quite convinced of having found it, I zigzagged between the puddles and turned on my flashlight. Its beam drew the washed-out blue postal sign out of the shadows. Solitary raindrops were dripping everywhere from the branches, the slot of the mailbox had been plastered with big, yellow, sopping wet leaves by the storm. It was impossible that this quaint little house stuck in the dead season could provide any news. Nevertheless, I pulled the chain hanging alongside the gate leading to the little garden: a big convent bell woke up behind the wall, sounding the alarm in the dense beech grove. Intimidated by the racket, an involuntary reflex made me huddle against the wall. As soon as the bell stopped ringing, the rumble of the gunfire again filled the street; now that the wind was no longer blowing, its noise alone seemed to ripple ever so slightly the water standing in the puddles. After three or four minutes, I saw a trembling light come on behind the blinds of a window on the first floor, unrelated, or so it seemed, to my ringing the bell: not really a response, but rather a sign of an absent-minded, dream-like winter night's insomnia manifesting itself. The light went out: I rang once more; it did not come on again. For a moment, I stood still among the puddles, disoriented, like someone whose plea for attention was met only by a silent stare from behind a ticket window.

Nothing prompted me to go back to the villa: I could not figure out why, but the sound of the bell had freed me of worries to do whatever I could, or ought to do; only one image captivated me now, held me in thrall: that of raked gravel underneath my feet and the lamp which would come towards me, while raindrops heavy as bullets fell from branches: everything stopped at the gesture of the bare arm holding the lamp up high, just as I had witnessed it in the salon, that slow, slightly solemn gesture made by someone who is showing off a treasure chest. Never before had I been so overwhelmed by the raw sentiment that someone was waiting for me.

I was thinking – or rather I let my thoughts run ahead of me on that path of confusion where I was stumbling along. Why had the meaning of an implicit avowal imposed itself so strongly as soon as I held the light up to the painting? And, at the same time, I could not help thinking that if my discovery had not been purposely desired, nothing at all – on the contrary – had been done to prevent it. How many years had she served Nueil, at that table, observed the same silence, performed the same ritual, her gestures and looks knotted into an oppressive yet tender uneasiness, which the painting condensed and consecrated like a mirror that recharges and captivates the face looking at itself? I thought about Nueil's sudden retirement. I imagined the last few summers at La Fougeraie just before the war, the silence, the varnished furniture creaking in the rooms – the heavy shadows around the villa, so much like the ardent, smoldering barrier of eyelashes lowered.

Leaving the side street where the post office was located, I continued to walk briefly on the road towards the village center. The idea of a return obsessed, and at the same time oppressed me; I needed time. My footsteps reverberated momentarily on the cobblestones, breaking the eerie silence rising from the fort-like row of tightly shuttered residences. But even the street's echo, the only sound reminding me that I was passing in front of one of those little houses, made me think of the villa: I could feel the thrill again caused by the sound of gravel suddenly crunching underneath her feet, in step next to mine. A humble servant, and yet calmly authoritarian – chained – but also putting others in chains. Day and night, it was her gestures that connected, tied together those tidy, polished rooms, gave expression to the silent captive's eloquent language so rich in strange communicative powers.

When the wind quiets down at nightfall and the rain stops after a daylong downpour, the streets of a village are like a woman who takes off her coat to reveal a summer dress; unencumbered, breathing easier, opening up. I passed in front of Braye's market hall, and walked for a rather long time, well beyond the short passage leading down to the train station, right up to where the houses were set further and further apart and the road again plunged into the forest. The clouds broke apart rapidly, two or three watery stars could be seen through an open space among the branches that covered the road like a ceiling. On the right, at the bottom of its trench, a short express train hurtled through the forest like a startled animal breaking out of its cover, scattering a layer of crumpled metallic shavings over the countryside. The night, cleansed by the rain, had once again become receptive to sounds; the noise left behind in the train's wake took a long time to die; reanimated by directional changes, it continued to reverberate in the woods at every bend in the tracks. I stopped for a moment to listen. The din made by angry gods far away was quieting down, making the oppressive night easier to bear: a yellow light flickered, then shone calmly in a window behind the branches, like a Queen-of-the-night flower opening. The line of gunfire on the horizon no longer troubled the silence any more than would the noise of a torrent in its mountain valley. There was a quiet and moist sweetness in the air. I kept on walking, feeling much lighter and more relaxed now that the storm had cleared. The image of the tall, steady flames of the candles in that closed room had come back to settle in my mind like in a hall of mirrors; it seemed as if the restored calm of the forest had crystallized around that light, lending an odd charm to the night.

The trees had formed a ceiling above the road; I kept on walking in a heavily dripping tunnel which no longer led anywhere; then I turned around. From time to time I thought of Nueil, almost absent-mindedly. The noise of the war could still be heard very far away, above the becalmed forest, woods so still now that one almost expected to see a ribbon of dawn's gray light rise momentarily behind them. I thought that it must be very late. Walking on the pavement now drained of water, I felt like someone who returns home after a sleepless night, and senses that the houses alongside the road are already less opaque, aired out from the light sleep of the early morning hours. I tried to slow down, but found myself walking briskly into that night so perfectly still but where, in some deep recess, something tender and sad was quietly burning.

The iron gates of La Fougeraie stood ajar; nevertheless, while walking towards the villa on the sand-covered courtyard I knew instinctively that no one had arrived; only one window towards the back of the house was dimly lit, its beam pulling the wall of a vine-covered coach house out of the shadows. I stopped for a few seconds in the middle of the courtyard, wondering whether I should knock on the pane of the lighted window. Alerted, the light left the vine-covered wall, started to glide from window to window towards the front steps. Moving along assuredly and without haste, indifferent to onlookers, without agitation or surprise, without any coquettish dawdling. Simply *this is how things are*. There never had been a need to announce oneself here.

The door opened silently while I was walking up the steps. Once again, I was struck by the somber, opaque image made by that tall silhouette outlined against the light, with features so difficult to identify; nothing but a lost profile receding into the darkness of the hallway, the shape of a cheek barely visible through the mass of black hair.

– No, she said, in response to my question silently formulated. – No one has come.

There was a singular tonelessness in her voice. Neither cold, nor frightened, nor resigned. Rather haughty and neutral, stating the obvious. No one had come, because it was no longer possible that anyone could show up.

Once again, I found myself alone in the music salon. I stretched out in the armchair and smoked for a while, silently, nervously. Even today, on a lone winter's night, it can happen that for a few moments I again put my elbows on the armrests of that chair just drifting along. The war-crazed world is closing in on me from all sides with the indifference of a cataract crashing down. Time flows sluggishly towards the darkest point of the dead season, life seems to recede in the ebb tide. But who cares! An ambiguous freedom is rising from behind that black rain on this disastrous day, like the dawn after a deluge where a dove's and a raven's wings might beat in unison. Nothing exists any longer except me, waiting – the night, all quiet now, is suddenly like a door that opens – through the mists rising from the dark earth, fallen leaves fly around me as far as the eye can see.

I waited. I felt incredibly awake. Candelabra in hand, I walked from one of the library sections containing music partitions to another. The silence of the plush carpet accentuated the unjustified character of my movements: suddenly, it seemed as if a shadow came and went with me in the salon: this was the start of that Parisian winter when so many bereaved families were beginning to sit down in circles at nightfall and silently join hands across a table: I turned around abruptly, fearful that I might be losing my mind. My nervousness became extreme. Where was she stirring now, all alone, in those somber regions deep inside the house? Behind the pretext of that silent, slavish deference shown to me since the afternoon, it seemed as though I was being treated in a rather strange way.

I replaced the candles that had almost burned down – unable to stay any longer in that haunted room, I started to walk through others just as empty and silent. In spite of the luxurious appointments, the prevailing atmosphere was so cold and uninviting that it felt awkward here to relax in an armchair: all the rooms seemed made for walking through, or remaining upright. The room where I dined had been restored to its frigid order. I suddenly had the feeling that everything experienced that evening was unreal: as I went from room to room, the doors seemed to close behind me, the objects returned to their fixed places automatically; there was no trace of myself passing through them, my presence was not being acknowledged. The painting still marked its somber spot on the wall, frozen in a museum-like solitude, irradiating the room like a small statue pierced with pins.

I started to go up one of the short stairways. The anonymity of the hallway where I found myself reminded me of a hotel's corridor – only larger, stuffier, impregnated by a heavy odor of wax. Down at the other end, a casement window cut out a pale rectangle from the obscurity. I drew the curtain aside and pressed my forehead against the windowpane. The night was not completely opaque; it had lost that cindery blackness of nights in the country: the air, filtered by the day's downpours, had taken on a crystalline transparency that brought obscure masses of the landscape so close to the window one was almost tempted to reach out and touch them. Beyond the clear space of the courtyard, the line of chestnut trees and the arbour were clearly visible: behind the supporting wall, the rounded, dome-like shapes of the trees growing in the ravine and on the adjoining plateau now stood motionless, arched against each other like heavy black bubbles, swollen by the fermentation of the spongy earth. The tree line detached itself from a gray stretch of sky illuminated by showers of tiny sparks, which seemed to originate very far away on the horizon. There was something wild, something savage about that surge of leafy masses: profiled against the backdrop of changing lights, they seemed to come to life, like a theater curtain whose folds begin to stir at the bottom just before it goes up. I opened the window halfway. Behind me, a tapestry was being slapped brutally against a wall in the hallway: the flames of the candles flickered very low. I took a deep breath of the fresh air blown in by the wind, almost relieved to hear the swishing noise that ran along and reverberated in the hallway like water rushing through the locks of a river. I closed the window. Furniture creaking ever so slightly, surfaces touching, brushing against each other, and many more sounds resonated at great length throughout the house: it was as though it had been stripped bare of furnishings. Cold, polished, wide open – singularly inhospitable. While returning to the salon, I had a momentary vision of Nueil sitting at his piano, with all the doors of the music room wide open. He is alone, his fingers on the keys pound the cold, sonorous emptiness, waking up the innermost regions of the house whose hall-ways seem to carry the noise like ear ducts, setting in motion a silent, rigid listening process. This special kind of silence, which the master of the house must have conjured up around him with his particular works, day after day, year after year, seemed to come back and permeate every room filled with the late-night calm: a house of few words and few signs, where the most familiar gestures, even those confined to the kitchen or pantry, were shielded by a greater silence and carried more weight than anywhere else, like in a convent's workroom or in a sacristy.

As soon as the clock struck eleven, the reflection of the light started to move on the ceiling of the hallway. Once again, I jumped up from my armchair. I no longer could imagine anything: nerves on edge, I watched the light on the hallway's ceiling come closer and closer. I no longer expected anything: throat constricted tightly, I waited with the utmost intensity; like a man in a dark cell who hears the sounds of footsteps outside his door. The light hesitated, then stopped for a second on the threshold, still hidden by the opened door; then the silhouette entered, in profile, and took two steps in my direction without turning to look at me, the raised arm again holding the candelabra silently in front of her.

I have seldom – perhaps never, even when in love – waited with such intense impatience and uncertainty – heart beating fast, throat tight – for someone who in this place could not be anyone for me except "a woman", – that is to say a question, a pure enigma. A woman about whom I knew nothing, neither the name nor roughly who she could be – not even her face, which could only be glimpsed stealthily, and thus kept all the uncertainty of a lost profile – nothing except that silent, cresting swell which momentarily took over the rooms and hallways while she glided in and out of them; it seemed to me that I would have recognized her among a thousand others by the ways in which the candlelight moved on the walls while she walked, as if carried along by a wave. But even in that instant of waiting, of heightened tension, when I could hardly control myself, I was struck by something special about that silhouette, which I had never seen except against a constantly obscured background, namely an extraordinary indistinctness. She seemed attached to the darkness surrounding her by some lifeline which sustained her entire being; the luxurious mane of black hair, the shadow obliterating the contours of her cheek, the dark clothes she wore at that moment did not differentiate her from, but rather made her one with, the night.

She was dressed in an ample dressing gown of a dark color held in at the waist by a cord, revealing only the tips of bare feet while she walked; her black hair, combed back, fell on the shoulders in a somber mass, its cascading tresses pulled up by a collar which rose high on her neck; her robe, more evening coat than dressing gown, fell from the waistline in rigid folds – hieratic, vaguely solemn, its elegance slightly understated but with just a hint of the theatrical, which rendered her servant's garb so intriguing – undressed for the night as one dresses for a ball.

Not one word was spoken. Ever since I had entered La Fougeraie, she imposed on me her ritual without words; she decided, she *knew*, and I followed. I was not even troubled, nor perplexed: just taken care of, pulled from moment to moment by a slender thread which I no longer thought of breaking. I followed her up the steps; the movement of the lights animated the entire staircase, illuminating one mirror, one shiny wooden panel after another so that the house, its every nook and cranny awakened by the tiniest spark of light, resembled a palace of mirrors. The narrow soles of her white feet swayed quickly back and forth in front of me from stair to stair like an ardent flame, poised for just an instant before immediately plunging again into the folds of that heavy fabric the color of soot: the rest of the silhouette moved with a somber, self-contained grace against the candlelight, the evening coat undistinguishable from the thick, animal-like black tresses cascading from her small head. The swaying movement of that torch up ahead pulled me silently in its wake, it was as if her feet never touched the ground, swept upward by a draft of wind; we kept on walking on that plush carpet without making the slightest noise. The blood was beating in my ears, and yet it seemed to me as though I was a spectator at that silent ascension. I desired her. I now knew that I had desired her from the first moment I saw her, as soon as my step next to hers set the gravel crunching in the courtyard. But at this moment such a detail was hardly of any importance. Nothing mattered except that constant tension constricting my neck, and that wind which seemed to whip her robe around her ankles all the way up the staircase.

She put the candelabra on an antique chest pushed against the wall next to the bed and remained standing for a moment, tall against the light, her head bent slightly forward. The room, seen through the fluttering of the candlelight, appeared to be full of shadowy corners, but nevertheless gave an impression of being intimately inhabited: a feminine room decorated with light-colored chintz curtains, and a dressing table whose mirror every so often would catch sparks of light, illuminating the back of the room. The almost aggressive modernism of the rooms on the ground floor ended at the door of this room; the massive, carved furniture with its spiraling columns, dark-colored and shiny, made one think of ancient Spain; the intimate, light-colored touches did not really match, they seemed to have been added here and there hastily, like a feminine nest attached haphazardly, clinging precariously to the sharp angles of raw oak. The posts of the canopied bed cast a structure of long shadows against the wall. There was nothing in the room to make me feel welcome; on the contrary, it seemed singularly distant at that moment, devoid of the tender imagery associated with a woman who is about to undress, but an appropriate setting for the severe-looking evening coat in which once again she seemed to officiate. I put my hands on her shoulders after sliding them inside the half-opened evening coat: they were bare; she lowered her head even more, the mass of her hair fell forward, covering her face like a curtain. This face, averted for the last time as if hidden behind a barrier, intimidated me; I did not dare try to kiss her lips, only her shoulder. She made not a single movement; did not defend herself, nor respond to me, I did not feel the surge of warm flesh against my mouth; there was neither surprise, nor waiting, nor urgent passion. Simply *this is how things are.* Head still bent forward, she only untied the cord around her waist with a precise movement of her fingers; once again, silently, proudly, she was assisting me.

All through that night we did not exchange a single word. The pleasure she gave me was brief and violent, but my memories remain a colorless blur, almost devoid of a sense of intimacy: nothing but that long body which seemed to come alive far away from where I was, eyes closed, gathering itself around a secret image, those noble legs which, during moments of pleasure, again seemed to animate the folds of the evening coat – that haughty docility, that distance which nothing could bridge. The slanting light of the candles cast shadows black as ink across the crumpled bed from which emerged a breast, a knee, the fold of a hip – the face stayed hidden, turned to the other side of the bed, craftily seeking again the shelter of her tresses. In a moment of anger, annoyed by that trembling light which made her look as if she were downing among the folds of the sheet, I brutally crushed her body with mine, immobilizing her against me with arms held rigid, but the body did not tense up, nor did it respond; it remained relaxed, in a state of surrender, without any sign of reaction. I felt a sort of panic, and almost reached out to strike that face so obstinately kept hidden from me. And then, almost immediately, I dropped off into a heavy sleep.

The night must have been almost over when I woke up; a feeble light, like a wintry dawn, projected the squares of the windowpanes across the curtains. I got up, and pulled one of the curtains back for a moment. Daylight was still far away, but the storm had subsided. The moon's crescent stood high above a vast, vacant expanse of sky, casting a thin white halo around the bulky fair-weather clouds gliding along much slower now.

Behind the gate, one could see distinctly the trodden path that had led me here, now drained and almost dry between the twin rails of water standing in its ruts. On the other side of the walk rose a low wall topped by an iron fence interrupted by a small gate, and, behind it, masses of trees belonging to another park. The air, cleaned by the rain, kept a glass-like transparency pleasant to the eye: one almost expected to hear a dog barking to test the sound's clarity: the rumble of the gunfire had not stopped, but diminished in volume, and no longer thundered like a cataract; it seemed to erupt in spasms, like a fire about to go out, against the background of an irregular drumbeat struck with muffled blows; a rumble that gave the impression of being closer, less obsessive. The night, now wide-awake and calm, with signs of fair weather ahead, tempted me to leave the house; for a moment I toyed with the idea of going outside to take a random stroll on paths once again dry and resonant, but then I returned to the bed and very quietly lit one of the candles. The feeling of security emanating from that night had calmed me – my train of thoughts took a new turn. Raising the candelabra slightly, I illuminated the other side of the bed. I looked at her, beset by a feeling of troubled, undefined anxiety. She was asleep, stretched out like a well-behaved child, lying flat on the bed, the head turned slightly to the other side, half of her face still covered by a mass of hair. One arm stretched outside to pull back the sheet had left a breast bared; a few tiny beads of perspiration in the folds of the neck and around the mouth caught the shine of the candlelight. An invisible weight seemed to hold her down on the sheets and pillow like some nocturnal force, as if to make her sink deeper into sleep than anyone else, sleep without a worry, without a thought, without restlessness. The night, now that the rain had stopped, brought closer the rumbling of the cannon and made me think again of Nueil, but that thought was not as oppressive as it had been during the evening: the calm after the storm had chased away the bad ghosts, cast aside the thought of death. One by one, the evening's images came alive in my mind, but now that the anguish which had constricted my throat was subsiding, I was able to reconsider those anxieties in a much harsher light, review what had happened against the background of a more critical, sharper chiaroscuro. I thought about the assured manner, so difficult to explain, which had set the tone during that strange ritual the night before, entirely orchestrated by her from beginning to end. I remembered the expression caught on her face the moment I opened the door to that dark room; rather than anxiety, it now seemed to have been some kind of dread. As if it had been out of the question – for him as well as for her – that Nueil could show up. As if I had been, from the very start, all throughout the performance of those unusual services – at the table, in bed – present and necessary, and yet intimately, peacefully, excluded.

— And yet . . . — a thought crossed my mind for an instant, but I immediately reconsidered; no, it seemed to have been pure expediency; I was not really shocked, but rather intimidated by that body sprawled across the sheet, which even in its sleep never lost its haughty indifference but remained, even at a distance, so intimately the prisoner of a gaze. I raised the candelabra a little higher and bent over her. Looking at her this way seemed as though I was watching myself bending over her, entering into a painting, becoming the prisoner of an image, perhaps in a spot assigned to me by some singularly odd powers-that-be. At that minute, she could not have been asleep. Suddenly, I visualized quite clearly the loaded airplane flying in the midst of its roar high up in the starry night, its course charted by readings of the earth down below punctured by fires and lined like a map by the criss-cross network of piano strings — the dust-encrusted bulk of the pilot, barely awake,

wrapped in his shawls and furs, the face illuminated from below, not so much by the lights of the
instrument panel as by the fixed image of that
woman, appeasing yet cruel, perhaps the only image where she could again take shape and live only
for him.

I looked, deep in thoughts, at the enigmatic
sleeping woman. My imagination now took me
back haphazardly through the years gone by.
Everything could not have been invented in that
strange scenario. Something whispered in my
ear – a hint of poverty, of dependency, an air of
false deference in her demeanor as soon as the
scaffolding of studied gestures fell away – that she
really had been Nueil's servant. Perhaps he wanted
only to live again, through others, a lost enchant-
ment: to be dazzled by beauty bestowed on him
unexpectedly in his house from behind an apron.
She, on the other hand, might be looking for yet
another confirmation of a feeling that must have

seemed almost magical to her, like a power. Because that role she played was only half an act: I knew she was not playing it coldly.

I stayed awake next to her for rather a long time. Looking intensely at a woman asleep conjures up around her an innocence, an aura of security bordering on folly: I never could fathom how one could abandon oneself in that manner, eyes closed, to another person's gaze. The gunfire had by now been reduced to sporadic volleys, and during the intervals of deep silence I could distinctly feel the depth of the house's inner regions, sense the long stretches of tidy, polished rooms. The air must have become more brisk after the last downpour, because a cold draft was coming into the room, seeping down from the tall windowpanes still colored blue by the night. This early morning hour was cold and clear; being able to order my thoughts with a cool head, in the slightly hostile detachment that comes with the end of desire, gave me a feeling of calm possession, of indulgent domination. Awake, looking at her asleep, like a book wide open on the chapter of her fraud, I felt no resentment, only a mysterious curiosity. Little mattered her ways, her reasons. There were no accounts to be rendered, neither by her nor by me. Simply: *this is how things are*; having started to walk down a road she had opened for me, I still was not sure where it led. In any case, ending in a shortcut that precluded any response, explanation, remorse, justification, words. The silence she had maintained all along cast on that night a purity still intact, a powerful charm. I was thinking that one could follow Orpheus very far in the somber kingdom, as long as he did not turn around. She never turned around. I had followed her. Even now I was still following her, almost, protected from every faux pas as long as I followed in her footsteps – strangely cared for, strangely charmed. For a moment, my gaze swept over the walls of the room. Night made it look spacious and light. I listened for a moment to her quiet and even breathing. Then I again lay down next to her, my hand seeking hers which rested on the sheet – a hand barer, fresher than her body – blew out the candles, and went to sleep.

When I woke, the place next to me was empty, the curtains opened; the early sun's wet haze flooded the room, birds were singing. A morning so dazzling that I rushed to open the window. The air was of a baptismal freshness; a slight breeze spread the green odor of fallen leaves. Life had returned to its old order; an invisible cart was bouncing along on the leafy path next to the park; the unmistakable sound of dishes clattering came floating up from the backyard. I had a sudden vision of her entering the room – an image I would never be able to outlive – apron tied around her waist, white bonnet holding her hair neatly in place, open arms carrying the breakfast tray. I got dressed in a panicky haste, hurried down the stairs and out into the courtyard. As soon as the gravel started crunching under my feet, the noise of the dishes stopped, but I did not look back. I walked quickly, teeth clenched, eyes downcast, looking at the sand on the ground. I closed the gate behind me without turning around. The carpet of leaves covering the dried path was soft to walk on, all along the road the villas set among the trees emerged one by one in the morning light, washed clean, looking like new. Only a milk seller's wagon rumbled up and down the leafy alleys, ringing its bell from time to time in front of the gates leading to deserted parks. The sun was shining through the canopy of branches above me; I walked quickly: while crossing the heart of the village, shutters were opening, clanging lazily against the facades, pails of water thrown on the sidewalks to rid them of layers of fallen green leaves. I remembered that it was All Souls' Day. But the anguish that weighed on me so heavily the night before had vanished; I walked into a tiny cafe in the midst of a stand of trees that was just opening its doors underneath a sign shaped like a pinecone, and ordered coffee. A parenthesis had closed, but it left in its wake something tender and burning inside of me that only time could erase. Looking through the small windows, I saw the forest at this early morning hour: something besides the rain had refreshed it, tamed it, just as if life had opened up for a moment, revealed itself in a close-up. It was going to be a beautiful day; and I thought that today, all day long, it would still be Sunday.